When Mama Retires

BY

Karen Ackerman

ILLUSTRATED BY

Alexa Grace

ALFRED A. KNOPF   NEW YORK

To Ben with love, and for Lee a.k.a. "the droop"
—K. A.

For my family and for a world without war
—A. G.

THIS IS A BORZOI BOOK PUBLISHED BY ALFRED A. KNOPF, INC.

Text copyright © 1992 by Karen Ackerman. Illustrations copyright © 1992 by Alexa Grace.
All rights reserved under International and Pan-American Copyright Conventions. Published in the United States
by Alfred A. Knopf, Inc., New York, and simultaneously in Canada by Random House of Canada Limited, Toronto.
Distributed by Random House, Inc., New York.
Book design by Mina Greenstein   Manufactured in Singapore   10 9 8 7 6 5 4 3 2 1

Library of Congress Cataloging-in-Publication Data
Ackerman, Karen, 1951–   When mama retires / by Karen Ackerman : illustrated by Alexa Grace.   p.   cm.
Summary: Henry, Will, and Charley learn to do things around the house when Mama considers retiring from
housework and becoming a wartime riveter.
ISBN 0-679-80289-4 (trade)   ISBN 0-679-90289-9 (lib. bdg.)
[1. House cleaning—Fiction. 2. World War, 1939–1945—United States—Fiction.]   I. Grace, Alexa, ill.
II. Title.   PZ7.A1824Wh   1992   [E]—dc20   91-19139

$\mathcal{M}$AMA peeks out through the gingham curtains, and we hear her murmur, "One of these days, I'm going to retire from housework, and things will change around here."

Henry, Will, and I look outside too and see our neighbor, Mrs. Phelps, leaving for work in gray factory overalls.

"If Jean can get a job at the war plant, so can I!" Mama declares, tucking in the corners of the kerchief she wears over her hair on cleaning days.

"What kind of job, Mama?" I ask.

We giggle at that idea, and Mama gives us one of her "There's a war going on" looks. She picks up our pajamas from the floor and tosses them in the wicker clothes basket. "It's time I taught you boys how to do some things around here," she says.

I hear Henry grumble, so I remind him how we promised Dad we'd pitch in and help while he was overseas in the Army.

Mama carries the clothes basket out to the washtub on our back porch, and we follow right behind. She fills the tub with hot water and pours in some soap flakes.

"You don't have to be an Einstein to do the wash," she explains, turning the handle that makes the clothes swirl around. We nod. But we wish we were Einsteins anyway.

After Mama rinses the clothes, she shows us how to turn the crank on the wringer and squeeze the water out. Henry and Will start cranking and look surprised when everything comes out flat as a flapjack. Then I roll the clothes up and put them back in the basket.

    We know what's next when Mama opens the door to
the backyard, where a rope clothesline stretches between
two big trees.
    Henry helps me push the laundry basket past the
scrap-metal box, while Will carries the sand bucket filled
with clothespins. Nearly every backyard has a box to
collect scrap metal, used to make machines for the war.

So far, ours has empty cans, Henry's broken pogo stick, one silver roller skate, a bent wheel from my bicycle, and an old tin breadbox in it. As we follow Mama down the line, I try to imagine how she'd look carrying rivets instead of clothespins.

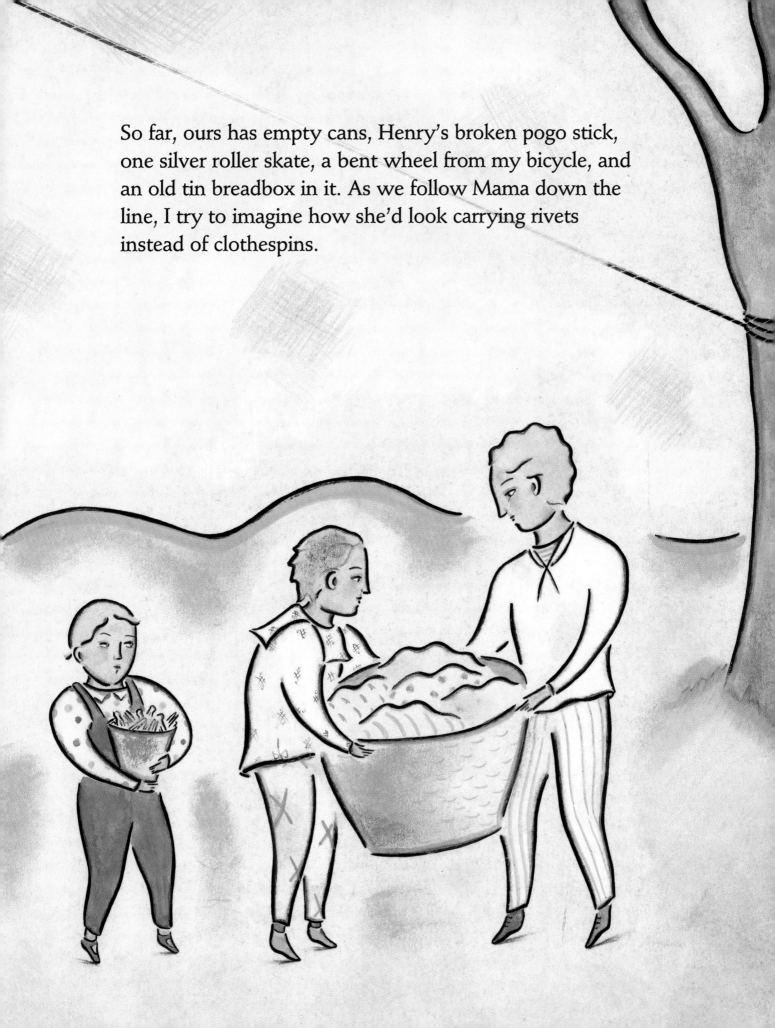

Some kids playing a game of stickball call out "Hi!" and "Come over!" I wave to them through the clothes flapping in the breeze. "We can't—we're pitching in!" I answer, and Mama smiles at me.

She leads us back inside and up the stairs to our room, then stops at the doorway, shaking her head. We sort of slink around, picking up dirty socks, toy PT boats, model bomber planes, and Dick Tracy comics, with "We're sorry" looks on our faces.

"Under the bed too, Charley," Mama tells me. I find two crumpled candy wrappers and my Scout cap. "Now that wasn't so hard, was it?" she asks, and I have to admit it wasn't.

At lunchtime, we go down to the kitchen. Mama takes eggs and a brown paper package of bacon from the icebox. She peels off half a dozen strips and puts the rest away.

"No more until the new ration book comes," she says with a sigh. Every family has a book of ration stamps to buy their fair share of food with, so there's enough left for soldiers like Dad to have extra helpings.

"You already know how to set the table," Mama reminds us. We lay out our plates, silverware, and cups, but we can't remember which side the forks or spoons go on. But Mama doesn't seem to care about forks or spoons. "Perfect!" she says as she brings over our bacon and eggs.

After lunch, Mama pulls the footstool up close to the sink. We take turns washing the dishes while she dries. The radio is switched to a Big Band station, and Mama sings along to "Mairzy Doats." When it's time, all three of us shout, "A kiddle-dee-divy-too-wooden-shoe!"

"Boogie Woogie Bugle Boy" comes on next, which starts us jitterbugging across the kitchen floor.
"Hey, Mama—watch me!" Henry squeals.

"Hay is for horses, Henry," she corrects, laughing, then gives him an extra spin.

Next, Mama gets the rug sweeper and three cotton rags from the hall closet. She puts a dab of oil soap on each rag, and we follow her from room to room, wiping dust from the furniture whenever she says, "Wipe!" Soon everything looks squeaky clean and smells lemony.

Henry and I take turns pushing the rug sweeper. The roller brush on the bottom spins, and the lint disappears inside. Even though he's little, Mama lets Will have the last turn. She tries not to notice when he bumps into the walls.

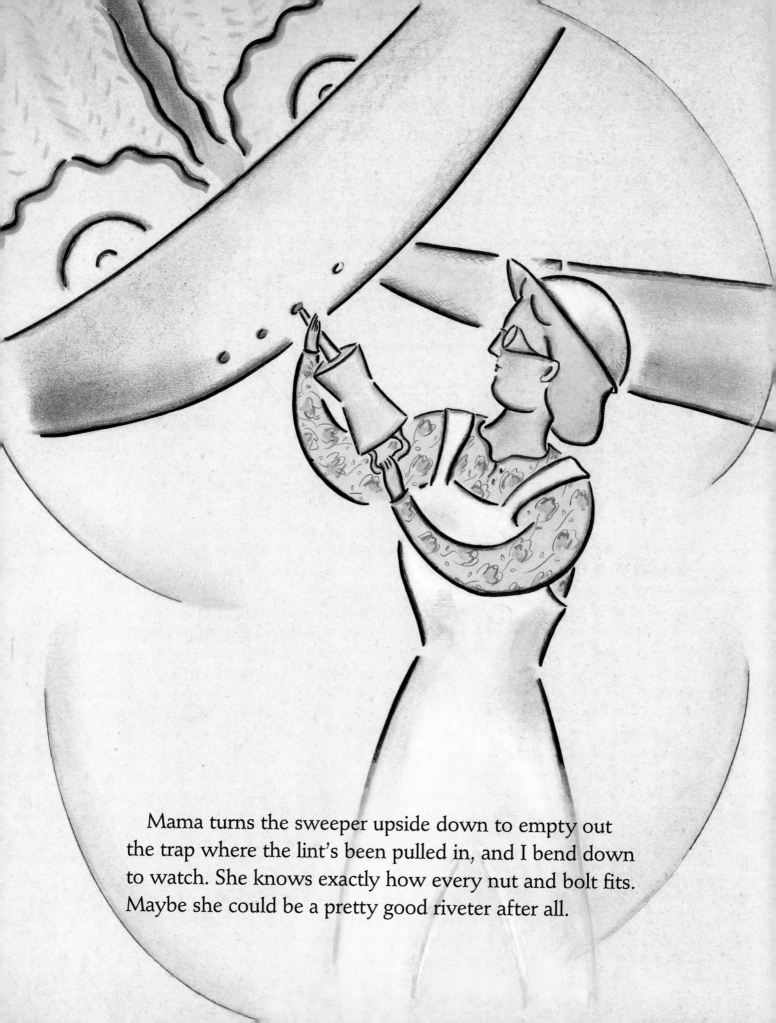

Mama turns the sweeper upside down to empty out the trap where the lint's been pulled in, and I bend down to watch. She knows exactly how every nut and bolt fits. Maybe she could be a pretty good riveter after all.

When the afternoon is almost over, I hope there isn't much left to learn. Doing housework is hard, and I wonder if factory work is this hard too. Then Mama crooks her finger at us, and we follow her back up the stairs.

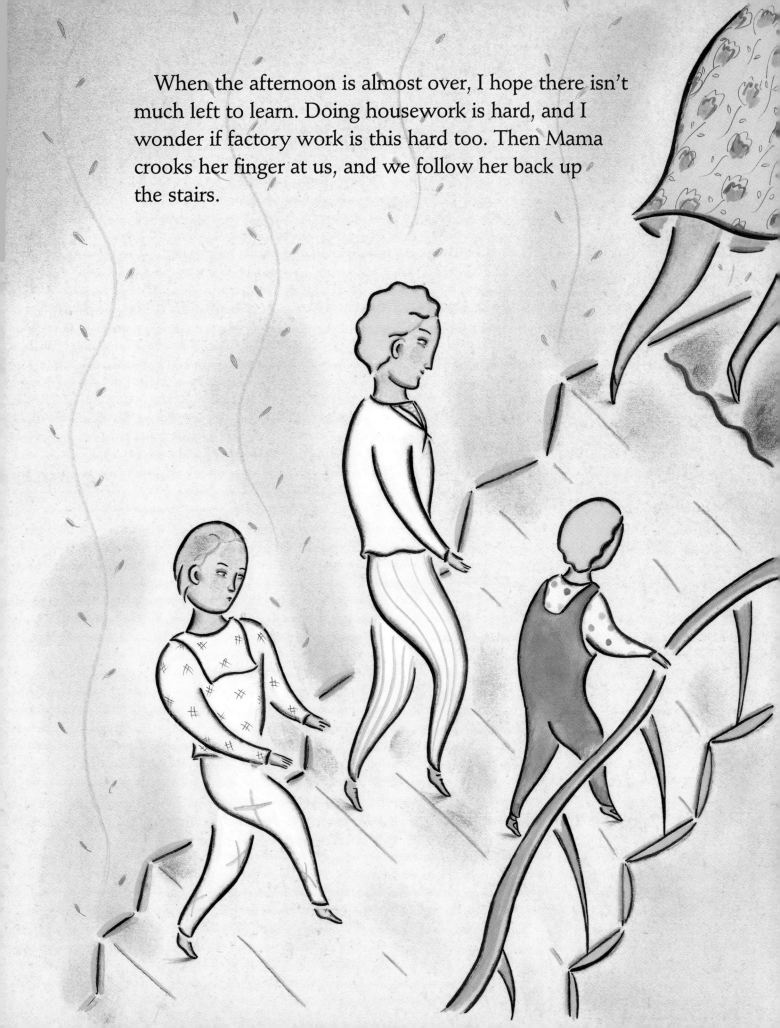

She lays a stack of clean, folded clothes on our dresser, and we put them away without being told.

Mama sits on my bed, watching us. When we're done, she pats the spot next to her, and we sit down. "I'm so proud of you," she says softly, giving each of us a hug. "And Dad would be, too."

"Will you still hug us when you retire?" Will asks.

"Mamas never, ever stop hugging!" she says, and squeezes him even tighter.

At last Mama lets us go outside, but the stickball game is already over. I sit on the front stoop and wipe the scuffs off my shoes, while Henry and Will try to walk-the-dog with their yo-yos. We practice what we learned to do in an air raid and listen for the roar of kamikaze planes in the sky.

As the laundry slaps on the clothesline, we wonder
where Dad is and what he hears.

"Is Mama really going to work in a factory, Charley?"
Henry asks in a whisper.

"I don't know," I tell him.

"Can we go with her?" Will asks.

"Kids aren't allowed."

Henry and Will move closer to me on the stoop. I try to remember how much soap goes in the wash, where the cotton dust rags are kept, and how to empty the rug sweeper.

Our shoulders touch. Henry and Will watch me, and when I move, they move too.

"It'll be okay," I tell them with a shrug.

But inside I'm hoping we'll be ready—when Mama retires.